THORPE, Kiki

Tink, north of
Never Land

Tink, North of Never Land

WRITTEN BY
KIKI THORPE

ILLUSTRATED BY
JUDITH HOLMES CLARKE,
ADRIENNE BROWN, & CHARLES PICKENS

HarperCollins *Children's Books*

First published in the USA by Disney Press,
114 Fifth Avenue, New York, New York, 10011-5690.

First published in Great Britain in 2007
by HarperCollins Children's Books.
HarperCollins Children's Books is a division of
HarperCollins Publishers,
77 - 85 Fulham Palace Road, Hammersmith, London, W6 8JB.

The HarperCollins Children's Books website is
www.harpercollinschildrensbooks.co.uk

978-0-00-722310-7
0-00-722310-2

1

Printed and bound in the UK

Visit disneyfairies.com

This boo̶ ̶ ̶ ̶ ̶ ̶ ̶ ̶ ̶ ̶ ̶ ̶ ̶ ̶ ̶ ̶ ̶od
from ̶ ̶ ̶ ̶ ̶ ̶ ̶ ̶ ̶

All About Fairies

IF YOU HEAD toward the second star on your right and fly straight on till morning, you'll come to Never Land, a magical island where mermaids play and children never grow up.

When you arrive, you might hear something like the tinkling of little bells. Follow that sound and you'll find Pixie Hollow, the secret heart of Never Land.

A great old maple tree grows in Pixie

Hollow, and in it live hundreds of fairies and sparrow men. Some of them can do water magic, others can fly like the wind, and still others can speak to animals. You see, Pixie Hollow is the Never fairies' kingdom, and each fairy who lives there has a special, extraordinary talent.

Not far from the Home Tree, nestled in the branches of a hawthorn, is Mother Dove, the most magical creature of all. She sits on her egg, watching over the fairies, who in turn watch over her. For as long as Mother Dove's egg stays well and whole, no one in Never Land will ever grow old.

Once, Mother Dove's egg *was* broken. But we are not telling the story of the egg here. Now it is time for Tinker Bell's tale...

Tink,
North
of
Never Land

1

"LAST ONE TO the meadow is a gooseberry!" Tinker Bell cried. "Terence, you don't stand a chance."

With a flap of her wings, Tink took off flying. It was early morning in Pixie Hollow. The air was cool and fresh. Below her, dew on the grass sparkled in the sunlight.

As she passed a patch of larkspur, the meadow came into view. She could see harvest fairies carrying armfuls of buttercups. A herd of dairy mice nosed through the grass, looking for seeds.

Tink glanced back at her friend Terence, a fairy-dust-talent sparrow man. He was way behind her. She turned and began to fly backward.

"A one-winged moth could fly faster than you!" she teased.

Terence grinned. But as he opened his mouth to reply, he saw something hurtling through the air. It was headed right for Tink!

"Tink!" he yelled. "Look out!"

Tink looked up. She dodged out of the way just in time.

As the thing zoomed past, Tink realised it was Twire, a scrap-metal-recovery fairy. Twire's arms were wrapped around a big metal object. She was struggling to stay aloft.

A second later, her wings gave out. Twire plummeted toward the ground.

"Twire!" Tink cried. She and Terence dove after her. But Twire was falling too fast. They couldn't catch up.

At the last second, Twire let go of the metal object. It slammed to the ground. Twire crashed next to it, just missing a dairy mouse. The mouse took off running with a frightened squeak.

Twire flipped once head over heels. She came to a stop flat on her back.

Tink and Terence rushed over. "Are you all right?" Terence asked.

The scrap-metal fairy rose shakily to her feet. Her elbows and knees were scraped, and one of her wings was bent. But her glow was bright with excitement.

"Look what I found," she said breathlessly, and pointed at the object. It was round and made of brass, with a glass front like a clock's. But instead of two hands, it had a single thin needle as long as a fairy's arm.

"What is it?" asked Terence.

Twire shook her head. "I don't know. I found it on the beach. But just look at all that brass!"

Twire's talent was collecting bits of unwanted metal and melting them down so that they could be remade into useful things. On a normal day, she picked up a few scraps of tin or a bucket that was rusted beyond repair. She rarely found such a large solid piece of brass.

Terence nudged the object with his foot. "It's awfully heavy," he said. "Why didn't you use fairy dust to carry it?" A sprinkling of dust could make almost anything float. Fairies often used it to carry heavy things.

"I did. I guess I didn't use enough," Twire admitted. She looked sheepish.

Twire always used as little fairy dust as possible. She couldn't help it, really. As a scrap-metal-recovery fairy, she was thrifty by nature.

Tink said, "I've seen one of these before. It's called a compass. Clumsies use them to keep from getting lost."

"Clumsies" was the fairies' name for humans. Tink knew about Clumsies from her adventures with Peter Pan. For years she had lived in his hideout and run wild with the Lost Boys. Those were some of her favourite memories.

"Compasses are very useful," she added, remembering what Peter had told her.

Twire looked dismayed. If the compass was still useful, she couldn't melt it down. "But this one's no good," she blurted out. "See how tarnished the brass is?"

"The brass doesn't matter. It's the needle that's important," Tink told her. "Whichever way you turn the compass, the needle always points north."

To show them, she began to turn the compass on the ground. Terence gave her a hand. They pushed the compass in a full circle. But instead of pointing north, the needle turned right along with the compass.

"It's broken!" Twire cried gleefully.

"I can fix it," Tink said.

Twire scowled at Tink. Tink met her gaze. Although the two were friends, they were often at odds. Tink always wanted to fix broken things. Twire, on the other hand, always wanted to melt them down.

For a moment, the two fairies glared at each other. Then, with a sigh, Twire said, "All right, Tink, it's yours." She took a last longing look at the brass and flew off to search for more metal.

When Twire was gone, Terence leaned in and pretended to examine the compass. He didn't really care about it, though. He just wanted to be close to Tink.

Terence liked Tink. He admired her dimples and her springy blond ponytail. He marveled at her talent for fixing pots and pans. In fact, he thought it was the best talent next to fairy dust. He loved Tink's smile, but he didn't mind when she frowned. Frowns were part of Tink, too. Above all, Terence liked that Tink was always herself. There was no other fairy like her.

Now Tink placed her hands on the compass. Her wings quivered with excitement. She had never fixed anything like it before. But she knew she could. She was the best pots-and-pans fairy in Pixie Hollow.

"Want me to help you take the compass to your workshop?" Terence asked. Tink nodded.

Terence sprinkled the compass with fairy dust. Then he remembered Twire's crash landing and added an extra pinch for safety. Together, Tink and Terence lifted it into the air.

They reached Tink's workshop, carrying the compass between them. But the fairy-sized door was a problem.

When they tried to push the compass through, it got stuck. They shoved with all their might. But it was wedged in good.

"Now what?" asked Terence. He slumped against the brass side of the compass.

Tink thought for a moment. "I'll make it shrink," she said at last. The magic would be tricky. It wasn't usual pots-and-pans magic. But Tink was sure she could do it.

She threw more fairy dust on the compass. Then she closed her eyes. Terence stood by, ready to lend a hand.

Terence is sweet, Tink thought. *He would do anything to help a friend.* She recalled the time he had gone with her to Peter Pan's hideout to get a hammer she'd left there. He had known, without being told, that Tink needed his help. And he'd offered it without being asked.

He's also very talented, thought Tink. *He can measure out cupfuls of fairy dust without losing a speck. And he has a nice smile. His smile sparkles.*

With a start, Tink realised that she wasn't thinking about the compass. She was thinking about Terence.

Tink opened her eyes. She was looking right at him. Terence smiled.

Tink frowned and looked away. She turned so that her back was to him.

"Can I help, Tink?" Terence asked.

"I don't need help." Tink wished he weren't hovering so close. In fact, she suddenly wished he weren't there at all.

She closed her eyes again. This time,

she thought only about the compass. She imagined it getting smaller, the metal contracting, compressing…

The compass began to shrink. It was only a smidgen, but Terence was ready. As soon as he saw it change, he gave a hard shove. With a screech of metal against metal, the compass rolled free and into the room.

At once, Terence knew he'd made a mistake. The compass was rolling straight toward Tink's worktable, with its teetering pile of pots and pans. He darted forward to stop it.

As he did, his wings swept a small silver bowl off Tink's shelf.

The bowl spun across the floor, right into the path of –

"No!" Tink cried.

Crunch! The compass rolled over the bowl, which crumpled like paper.

Tink pushed past Terence. She picked up the crushed bowl and cradled it in her hands.

Terence began to apologise. "I'd fly backward – "

"Look what you've done, Terence!" Tink exploded. She was shaking with anger. "Wherever I turn, you're underwing. If you really wanted to help me, you'd leave me alone!"

Terence drew back as if he'd been slapped. Without a word, he turned and flew away.

TINK WATCHED TERENCE leave. She half hoped he would turn around and come back. But he didn't. Soon he was out of sight.

She frowned and tugged her bangs. Perhaps she'd spoken a little harshly, and a little quickly.

"But Terence *is* always in my way," she complained, trying to convince herself. "I can't even turn around without tripping over him. And now look what a mess he's made."

She examined the crumpled silver bowl. Flattened as it was, it looked more like a plate.

"There, there," Tink murmured. "I'll have you put right in no time."

She ran her fingers lovingly over the silver. Tink adored anything made of metal. But this bowl was particularly special. It was the first thing she'd ever fixed as a pots-and-pans fairy, just after she'd arrived in Never Land. She hadn't been sure she *could* fix it. And she was so pleased at the way it had finally turned out.

As soon as her tinker's hammer was in her hands, she relaxed. Before long, she was lost in her work. She almost managed to forget all about Terence.

As Terence flew through Pixie Hollow, he hardly saw where he was going. Tink's words kept running through his mind. He'd never known she felt that way. He'd been hanging around her for years. Had he been a bother the whole time?

"I'll leave Tink alone from now on," Terence vowed. The idea made him sad. But what else could he do? She didn't want him around.

These heavy thoughts weighed Terence down, until he was flying just inches above the ground. His feet brushed the tips of grass blades as he flew over them.

Without noticing how he'd gotten there, Terence came to Minnow Lake. The lake was really no more than a puddle. But to the tiny folk of Pixie Hollow, it seemed vast. Although they couldn't swim, many fairies and sparrow men went there to enjoy the sunshine or just to dip their feet in the cool water.

Terence flew straight over the lake. His toes kicked up a spray. His boots got soaked and he didn't even feel it.

Suddenly, something whipped by him in a blur. Terence looked up and saw the water fairy Silvermist. She was gliding across the top of the lake on one foot, as graceful as an ice-skater. Her long blue-black hair waved behind her like a banner.

Silvermist skated up to Terence, smiling. Right away, she noticed his gloomy expression.

"Why, Terence, what's wrong? You look as if you lost your best friend."

Terence looked at her in surprise. How did she know?

Silvermist didn't know. But like all water fairies, she was very sensitive. She could tell Terence was hurting.

"I know what would cheer you up. Water-skating!" she said. "Want to join me?"

Terence watched as she twirled. "Sure, but I don't see how," he replied. "Only water talents can walk on water."

"Wrong!" said Silvermist. She spun on her toes and sped away.

Moments later, she returned. In her hands was a pair of green sandals with wide flat soles. She handed them to Terence.

"Put these skimmers on," Silvermist instructed. "They're made from lily pads. They'll keep you afloat."

Terence eyed the lily pad skimmers doubtfully. But he strapped them on over his boots. Gingerly, he set one foot, then the other, down on the surface of the lake.

He was standing on water!

"Whoops!"

Terence's feet slipped out from under him. He caught himself with his wings before he fell into the lake.

"They take some getting used to," said Silvermist. "Try walking. It's easier than standing still. You can use your wings for balance."

Terence took a careful step. He was surprised to find that the water was springy. It felt like walking on deep moss.

He took another step. Then he took three giant steps, flapping his wings in between. Each time he set his foot down, it bounced off the water. Soon he was bounding around the lake.

For the first time since that morning, Terence smiled.

Tink stretched out the crick in her back and sighed happily. She had worked hard all afternoon. After she'd fixed the bowl, she had started on the compass.

"At this rate, I'll have it working again by tomorrow," she said.

She stood and flew out of her workshop. Outside, she headed toward the orchard. "I'll go pick a cherry," Tink said. "I'm feeling kind of hungry."

She followed the bank of Havendish Stream. As she passed Minnow Lake, Tink heard laughter.

That's Terence's laugh, she thought.

Suddenly, she remembered what had happened that morning. *Maybe I was a little mean*, thought Tink. After all, the bowl had been easy to fix. Tink shrugged. *Oh, well.* She'd give him a friendly smile and show him that all was forgiven.

She flew to the lake and landed at the edge. There was Terence, skipping across the surface of the lake like a water strider. Silvermist skated along beside him.

Tink waved at them from the shore. Silvermist didn't see her, but Terence did. He was about to wave back. Then he remembered his vow. He kept his arms at his sides.

Tink frowned. Hadn't they seen her? She waved again. This time she was sure Terence glanced in her direction. But he turned and skipped away.

Tink lowered her arm. "Well," she said at last. "I'm glad Terence found someone to play with, at least."

And with a toss of her ponytail, she went on her way.

3

THE NEXT MORNING, Terence was up early. As the first rays of sunlight warmed Pixie Hollow, he filled a gunnysack with fairy dust. Then he set off to make his rounds. His job as a dust talent was to make sure all the fairies and sparrow men of Pixie Hollow had enough dust to do magic.

As he flew, Terence tried not to think about Tinker Bell. But it wasn't easy. He passed cornflowers the colour of her eyes and buttercups as golden as her hair. By the time he came upon the light-talent fairy Iridessa, Terence had been unsuccessfully not-thinking about Tink for more than an hour.

At that moment, Iridessa was headfirst in a large day lily. The lily glowed from within like a giant orange lantern. Terence gently tapped Iridessa's foot to let her know he was there.

Iridessa shrieked and popped her head up. She had yellow pollen in her hair. More pollen was streaked across one cheek.

"Terence! You could scare the fairy dust off someone, sneaking up like that!"

"Wouldn't you know it?" Terence said with a sigh. "And it's my job to put the fairy dust on fairies." He scooped a cupful of dust from the sack and poured it over Iridessa. She shivered lightly as the dust settled on her.

"So, why are you collecting pollen?"

Terence asked. "Have you turned into a garden fairy?"

"Come on," she said to Terence. "I'll show you."

Iridessa grabbed the basket of pollen. She led Terence to a nearby clearing and told him, "Take a seat."

For a moment, Iridessa hovered, focusing. Then she held up her hands. She began to pull sunlight out of the air.

Terence looked on in wonder. Every fairy and sparrow man had a magical talent, and Terence loved his best of all. But he was always amazed by the magic other fairies could do.

When Iridessa was done, she and Terence were sitting in a halo of darkness. It was like the circle of light a camp-fire casts on a moonless night.

Only instead of a bright spot in the darkness, it was a dark spot in the daylight.

"Amazing!" Terence said.

Iridessa glanced at him. The sunlight she had gathered sat in balls at her feet. "That's not even the good part. But I need darkness, or you won't be able to see what I'm about to do."

She took some of the sunlight and formed it into a bubble. Then she filled the bubble with pollen from her basket. She drew her arm back and threw it into the air as hard as she could.

Terence watched the bubble of light travel up, up, up. It burst with a pop. Golden pollen rained down. It looked like fireworks. But there was no fire – only pollen, light, and magic.

Terence thought, I wish Tink could see this. "It's brilliant!" he told Iridessa.

She beamed at the compliment and threw two more pollen-filled bubbles into the air. They burst in golden sprays of light.

"Wait!" Terence sprang to his feet. "I have an idea. Try using fairy dust."

Iridessa formed another ball of light. This time, Terence filled it with dust from his sack.

The fairy-dust-filled bubble floated out of Iridessa's hands even before she could throw it. It rose all the way up to the edge of the darkness.

Just when Terence thought the bubble would drift into daylight and disappear, it exploded. Blue, violet, green, yellow, orange, red – the light shimmered with the bright colours of the rainbow.

Terence and Iridessa watched in awe, the sparkles reflected in their eyes.

"Got it!" Tink cried.

She stepped back and watched the compass needle swing around. She was sure she'd finally fixed it. As Tink turned the compass, the needle pointed north. She'd fixed it, all right.

She stretched her arms and sighed with pleasure. How she enjoyed seeing a job done right! She turned the compass a few more times, just to admire her work.

Gradually, though, Tink became aware that something was missing. She checked to make sure she had her tinker's hammer. Then she checked her other tools. They were all there.

She looked around her workshop. Everything seemed to be in its place. The extra rivets were in their hanging basket. The little jars of glue lined the window-sill in a neat row. The silver bowl was back on its shelf, right where it had been before Terence knocked it off.

Terence! Suddenly, Tink realised that he was what was missing. Usually he stopped by to visit. But she hadn't seen him all day.

He must be busy. After all, he has work to do, too, Tink thought.

"I'll drop by the fairy dust mill and see how he is," she said. The mill was where Terence spent most of his time.

Tink flew out the door. She followed the hill that sloped down toward the mill, which sat on the bank of Havendish Stream.

She flew through the mill's double doors. Inside, it was cool and dim. Tink saw several fairies and sparrow men at work. But Terence wasn't among them.

Tink flew back outside. She was surprised at how disappointed she felt.

As she made her way back to the Home Tree, Tink saw a spark of light float up from a nearby field. Another spark followed.

Fireflies? she wondered. No, that couldn't be right. Fireflies only came out at night. Tink flew over to take a look.

When she reached the field, she

stopped and stared. In the center was a small clearing. Though the sun shone brightly overhead, the clearing was as dark as night. Within the darkness, bursts of light bloomed like flowers.

Looking more closely, she made out two tiny figures on the ground. One was her friend Iridessa. Tink strained her eyes, then blinked in surprise. The other one was Terence! With each new explosion, he and Iridessa clapped an cheered.

Tink hovered at the edge of the darkness, feeling strangely left out.

4

THAT EVENING, Tink hurried to the courtyard of the Home Tree. The sun was already setting. Any minute, the story would begin. She didn't want to be late.

Dinner had just ended. It was time for the story-talent fairies to spin their tales. That night, it was Tor's turn, and Tor was one of Tink's favouriteite storytellers. He knew more about pixie lore than most fairies put together.

The courtyard was filling with fairies and sparrow men. Tink looked around for Terence. They usually sat together during stories.

More and more fairies arrived.

They settled onto toadstools around the courtyard.

Tink tugged her bangs. Where was Terence? If he didn't get there soon, all the good seats would be taken!

On the other side of the courtyard, Terence caught sight of Tink. The seat next to him was empty, and he wanted to call her over.

But we aren't friends anymore, he reminded himself.

As Terence hesitated, he heard someone call his name. He looked around. Rosetta, a garden fairy, was hovering behind him.

She pointed to the seat next to Terence. "Is someone sitting here?"

Terence shook his head.

Rosetta sat down. She carefully

smoothed her rose-petal skirt. She fluffed her hair. Then she crossed her dainty ankles and folded her hands in her lap. With her long auburn curls, rosy cheeks, and elegant wings, Rosetta was one of the prettiest fairies in all of Pixie Hollow. She knew it, too.

When she was finally settled, she turned to Terence. It was then that she noticed his sad expression.

"Ah!" Rosetta gasped in horror.

Terence leaped into the air. "What? What is it?" He thought maybe a fire ant had crawled onto his toadstool.

"You shouldn't frown like that. Your face could get stuck," Rosetta told him gravely. "It happened to a fairy I know. Her face got stuck in a frown, and after that she always looked as sour as a stinkbug. That's why I always smile. If my face ever gets stuck, at least I'll know I'll always look good." To prove her point, she flashed a brilliant grin.

Rosetta's advice was lost on Terence. He never thought much about how he looked. He did notice Rosetta's smile, though. It was so charming, he couldn't help smiling back.

At that very moment, Tink finally spotted Terence. Her mouth fell open in surprise. Terence hadn't saved her a seat after all. He was sitting with Rosetta. And they looked very happy to be together!

Tink felt a lump in the pit of her stomach. But before she could do anything, a hush settled over the crowd. The story was about to begin. Quickly,

Tink looked around. All the seats were taken.

"Pssst. Tink!"

Fawn, an animal-talent fairy, waved at her. "You can share with me," Fawn whispered.

Tink flew down and squeezed herself in next to Fawn. As she did, she noticed a stinky smell.

"What's that smell?" she whispered to Fawn.

"Oh, it's probably me! I was playing tag with some skunks," Fawn told her. "Didn't get a chance to take a bath."

Tink nodded and held her breath. At least she had a seat.

The storyteller Tor alighted in the center of the courtyard. He looked around with twinkling eyes. Then he began, "Long, long ago, before the Home Tree, even before Mother Dove, there was the Pixie Dust Tree."

Tink let out a small sigh. She knew the story of the Pixie Dust Tree well. It was one of her favouriteites.

"In those days, Pixie Hollow was a great land," Tor went on. "It stretched for miles. It covered mountains, forests, and rivers."

Tink mouthed the next words along with the storyteller: *Too many years ago to count.*

"The Pixie Dust Tree stood at the center of it all," said Tor. "The dust flowed endlessly from deep within its trunk. And because the dust was plentiful, so was the fairies' magic… "

As Tor spoke, the Pixie Dust Tree

seemed to take shape before the fairies' eyes. Tink saw every detail, from its spiraling branches to its sturdy roots. She could hear its leaves rustle. She could feel the breeze from the gusts of pixie dust that rose from its center. That was the magic of story-talent fairies. Whatever they described became, in that moment, real.

Tor's story wove a spell around his audience. The fairies saw Pixie Hollow as it once had been: purple mountains, crystal-clear streams, fields of sunflowers stretching as far as the eye could see. And everywhere, fairies flying, playing, and living happily.

Then, suddenly, the scene darkened. An evil force threatened the fairies' world. No storyteller would say its name out loud. They were afraid of calling it back again. So in Tor's story, it appeared as a black cloud casting its shadow over Pixie Hollow.

The fairies in the story knew their world was in danger. They used every bit of magic they had to protect it. But in the end, they couldn't save everything.

They watched helplessly as the dark cloud swallowed the Pixie Dust Tree.

As brave as Tink was, she always found that part of the story hard to bear. Without thinking, she closed her eyes and reached out her hand to Terence.

Her hand closed on nothing. Tink's eyes opened. She'd forgotten. Terence wasn't sitting next to her.

Tink looked around. Fawn's eyes

were wet. So were the eyes of other fairies.

"But in its place, the Home Tree grew," Tor told them. "Fairies came from all over Pixie Hollow to live in the tree and make it their home. It brought the Never fairies together. And we found Mother Dove, who gave us fairy dust again."

The fairies saw the image of Mother Dove. Her feathers shimmered. After the Pixie Dust Tree had been destroyed, fairies had learned to make dust from the magical feathers Mother Dove shed.

"The Pixie Dust Tree is long gone," Tor told them. "But a bit of its dust still remains. It hangs in a cloud just over the cliffs on the Northern Shore of Never Land. You can see it on certain nights."

A sparkling cloud seemed to hang in the air around the listening fairies. As they watched, it began to fade. Finally, it disappeared.

For a moment, the crowd was silent. Then one fairy sighed. Another stretched her wings. The spell was broken. The story was over.

The crowd began to rise from their seats. A few of the music talents struck up a melody. Some of the fairies stayed to dance. Others headed back to the tearoom, hoping to find dessert.

Tink heard Fawn's stomach growl. "Sad stories always make me hungry," Fawn explained. "Come with me to the tearoom?"

"Sure," said Tink. She glanced at Terence and added, "Maybe we should invite Terence and Rosetta, too."

"Good idea," said Fawn. "Rosetta hates to miss dessert."

Together they flew toward Terence and Rosetta. But just as they reached them, the music fairies began to play a lively tune.

Rosetta sprang up from her seat. "This is my favouriteite song. Let's dance, Terence!"

She grabbed his hands and pulled him into the air. In the wink of an eye, the two had danced away.

5

TINK WAS SO SURPRISED, her glow sputtered. She watched Terence and Rosetta twirl through the air. They didn't so much as glance in her direction.

I didn't want their company anyway! she thought. *I have better things to do than watch two silly fairies dance.*

Ignoring Fawn's surprised look, she whirled around and stormed off to her workshop.

Inside, she slammed the door behind her. When that didn't make her feel better, she kicked over the basket of rivets. They rolled to every corner of her tidy workshop, which only made Tink's temper worse.

"Every time I see Terence, he

ignores me!" she fumed. She paced in the air. "Why, he practically goes out of his way to avoid me. And he hasn't been by to visit since... since... "

Oh.

Tink sat down with a thump. Finally, it dawned on her: she'd told Terence to leave her alone, and that was exactly what he was doing.

All the anger went out of her like air from a bellows. Within seconds, it was replaced by regret.

I haven't been very nice to Terence, she thought with a sigh. Her shoulders slumped. Losing a friend felt terrible.

But she wasn't one to mope for long. In Tink's opinion, problems were like broken pots. There wasn't one that couldn't be fixed. She was, after all, the best pots-and-pans fairy in Pixie Hollow. Surely she could come up with a solution.

A moment later, she'd thought of one.

"I'll win back his friendship!" she exclaimed. "I'll show everyone what a good friend I am." The idea made her spring into the air with excitement.

"But how will I do it?" She began to pace again.

It never occurred to Tink to say "I'm sorry." Only Clumsies said that. She might have said, "I'd fly backward if I could." But that didn't occur to Tink, either. She was too busy thinking of bigger, flashier ways to show that she cared.

"I'll give him a present," she said. "Something rare and wonderful." Her mind swirled with possibilities. A pirates' gold doubloon? Or a bunch of Never blooms with blossoms that never wilted?

Tink shook her head. Those things were marvelous of course. But what would Terence care for a flower or a gold coin? No, she wanted to give him something that was right only for him.

Terence is a dust talent, she mused. *He loves fairy dust as much as I love pots and pans.* But she couldn't give him fairy dust. He already had all the dust he could ever want.

Or did he? Tink remembered the end of Tor's story: "The Pixie Dust Tree is long gone. But a bit of its dust still remains. It hangs in a cloud just over the cliffs on the Northern Shore of Never Land."

That was it! Pixie dust was just like

fairy dust, only it came from a tree instead of Mother Dove. She could bring Terence dust from the Pixie Dust Tree!

Tink imagined how Terence's face would look when she gave him the last pixie dust in the world. How impressed he would be!

The Northern Shore was far from Pixie Hollow. It might take her days to get there, and the journey was sure to be rough. But the challenge only made Tink more excited.

"I'll leave tonight," she said. "I'll need to bring food. And extra fairy dust to fly – "

Tink's eyes fell on the compass. Of course. She could take it with her. It would point her right to the Northern Shore. How wise she'd been to save the compass from Twire's scrap pile!

She began to pack, piling things on top

of the compass – a sweater, a canteen, a sack of dried blueberries, a wool blanket, her spare dagger, a waterproof pouch to store her fairy dust in, some biscuits, a tin cup, a bag of tea...

Tink stepped back. The heap of things towered nearly to her chest. How in Never Land was she going to carry it all?

She snapped her fingers. "A balloon carrier!"

Balloon carriers were large fairy-dust-filled balloons with hanging baskets. Fairies used them to carry heavy loads. Some were big enough to carry fifty fairies. Others were quite small, just the right size for a fairy, a compass, and a few other odds and ends.

She knew she shouldn't take a

balloon carrier without telling anyone. But she was afraid that if Queen Clarion heard of her plan, she would forbid Tink to go. *Besides,* Tink reasoned, *if other fairies knew, it might ruin the surprise for Terence.* Fairies were terrible at keeping secrets.

"I'll be gone for just a few days," she said. "I'm sure the others won't even miss it."

Tink knew that the laundry fairies kept small balloon carriers anchored to roots inside the laundry room. The problem was getting one without anyone noticing.

"I'll have to borrow it after everyone goes to bed," she whispered to herself.

So, drawing her little stool up to the window, Tink settled down to wait.

6

THE MOON WAS high in the sky. The Home Tree was dark and silent. Even the fireflies that lit Pixie Hollow at night had blinked out.

As quietly as possible, Tink loaded the balloon carrier. Then she picked up the carrier cord and rose into the air. She circled the Home Tree, careful not to snag the balloon on low branches.

She flew over the barn where the dairy mice slept, and continued up, until she was above the tree line. She skimmed along the tops of the trees. Every few minutes, she darted back to look at the compass. She loved to see the needle pointing north, telling her exactly which way to go.

She'd been flying for a quarter of an hour when she looked down. Her heart sank. She was just crossing Havendish Stream.

At this rate, it will take me weeks to reach the Northern Shore! she thought.

But as luck would have it, the wind shifted in Tink's direction. She felt the carrier bumping against her heels.

Tink climbed into the basket. She let the wind speed her along. In no time, she had reached the edge of Pixie Hollow. Never Land's forest spread out below her like a great dark sea.

A moth flew up to the basket. It danced around Tink, drawn by her glow. She waved her arms, and the moth flew away.

Tink leaned back. High overhead,

stars winked in the black sky. The basket gently rocked her. Her eyelids grew heavy.

Within moments, she fell fast asleep.

Tink awoke with a start. The balloon had stopped moving.

She peeked over the side. The ropes that held the balloon to the basket were tangled in the branches of a large oak. The balloon must have drifted too low while she had been sleeping.

Tink climbed out of the basket and landed on a branch. She began to tug at the ropes.

Something snuffled behind her. She whirled around. A pair of red eyes stared at her from the darkness.

Tink gasped and sprang into the air.

Through the leaves of the tree, she could see more creatures in the branches around her. Each way Tink turned, she saw another pair of glowing eyes. She was trapped!

One of the creatures began to move along a branch toward her. Taking a deep breath, Tink flared her glow like a flame, hoping to scare it away.

It worked. The creature hissed and retreated to the other end of the branch. By the light of her brightened glow, Tink saw the long, pointed nose of a possum.

Tink tried to remember everything she knew about possums. They didn't eat fairies – did they? Fawn had once told her a story about a possum, though Tink couldn't recall the details. Oh, why hadn't she paid more attention!

One thing Tink did know was that she was still in trouble. The possums were bigger than she was, and she had dropped into their home. If they felt threatened, Tink was in danger.

Cautiously, Tink landed again on the branch. Keeping an eye on the largest possum, she began to pull at the tangled ropes. Every time a possum moved, she flared her glow.

Just as Tink grabbed the last rope, she heard a low growl. The largest possum had made up her mind. She didn't want Tink in her tree.

The possum bared her sharp teeth. Tink gave a desperate tug, and the rope came free. Quickly, she grabbed the carrier cord. She darted toward an opening in the branches, dragging the balloon.

The noise of the balloon crashing through the leaves startled the possums. They drew back just enough to make a path. Tink flew out of the tree and kept on going.

High above the forest, Tink stopped. She climbed into the basket and huddled there, shaking. Flaring her glow had used up all her energy.

Tink drifted in the balloon. She didn't care where the breeze took her, as long as it was away from the oak tree. But luck was once again on her side. When she checked the compass, she saw she was still headed north.

For the rest of the night, Tink pinched herself to stay awake. She was afraid to doze off again. When the wind changed direction, she got out and flew. Always she followed the compass needle to stay on course.

At last she saw a thin red glow on the horizon. Tink guided the carrier down to the edge of a small clearing. She tied the cord to a tree root to anchor it.

Under the shelter of a wild rosebush, she unrolled her blanket. She plucked a blossom to use as a pillow and curled up on a leaf.

Finally, she slept.

7

THE SUN HAD been up for hours when Tink opened her eyes. She heard the sound of waves breaking on a beach.

I must be near the ocean, she thought sleepily.

In an instant, she was wide-awake. The sound could mean only one thing. She had reached the Nothern Shore!

But how was that possible? Tink wondered. Surely the Northern Shore was still at least a day's flight away. She darted up into the air, until she could see over the tops of the trees. Blue-green water shimmered in the distance.

"The ocean!" cried Tink.

She raced back to her camp and checked the compass needle. It pointed toward the water. She did a joyful little dance. She *had* made it to the Northern Shore!

Quickly, she ate a dried blueberry and washed it down with water from the canteen. Then she packed everything into the basket and took off through the forest.

The sound of the surf grew louder. Up ahead, she caught glimpses of blue sky between the trees.

"Almost there!"

She emerged into sunlight. For a moment, she hovered, blinking. After the shady forest, the brightness was blinding. Over the splash of the waves, she could hear a different noise, like a melody.

It sounds as if someone is singing, thought Tink.

As her eyes got used to the light,

Tink looked around. Soft white sand stretched a mile in each direction. Blue water gently lapped the shore. Coconut palms rustled in the breeze.

Tink thought, *This beach seems familiar...*

Then she saw it. Straight out at sea, a large seaweed-covered rock rose from the water. A lovely woman sat on top. Her long tail with glistening scales curled down one side of the rock.

Tink's heart sank. The creature on the rock was a mermaid. And the song she heard was a mermaid's song. She hadn't reached the Northern Shore at all. This was Mermaid Lagoon, less than an hour's flight from Pixie Hollow.

Tink flew circles of fury. "But how?" she wailed. She had checked the compass over and over again. Always she'd gone north, in the direction the needle pointed. So how had she come to Mermaid Lagoon? Everyone in Never Land knew that it was on the opposite side of the island –

Tink dropped to the ground. How could she have been so stupid? Of course, a compass would be worthless on Never Land. For although a compass always pointed north, the island turned in whatever direction it wanted. Unlike most islands, Never Land floated freely in the ocean.

The night before, as Tink had flown doggedly north, Never Land had turned itself around. So she had ended up back where she'd started.

"Northern Shore. What a stupid name!" Tink growled. "Whoever thought it up should be pinched black and blue. And as for this piece of junk – "

In a fit of rage, Tink hauled the compass out to sea and threw it in. With a splash, it vanished beneath the waves.

Tink flew back to shore and flung herself down on the sand. She shook off the urge to cry.

"I won't give up," she told herself. "I'll get to the Northern Shore if I have to fly for a week."

Tink was like the pots she fixed – she had a will made of iron. She had never failed before. And she wouldn't this time, either.

Her mind made up, Tink stood and reached for the carrier cord. But it wasn't there. She spun around. The carrier was nowhere in sight.

Looking up, she spotted it high in the sky. In her rage over the compass, she had forgotten to tie it down. As Tink watched, the carrier drifted over the top of a towering palm tree and was gone.

Tink clutched her head in horror. She'd lost an entire balloon carrier! What would the queen say if she knew? What would Terence think?

But the carrier wasn't all she'd lost. Her food was gone, and so was her water. She'd have to find her own from here on. Luckily, she had kept her fairy dust with her. It was in a pouch on her belt. Tink checked her supply. She figured she had four days' worth, at least.

Now she was more determined than ever to find the dust from the Pixie Dust Tree. She had to prove that her journey had been worth it.

She set off flying through the woods. It was easier traveling by day. She knew that as long as she kept Torth Mountain on her right, she was headed the right way.

Tink flew all morning. When her shoulders ached too much to go on, she stopped beside a small spring. She took a long drink of cool water. Then she sat back to rest.

She thought about the journey ahead. She would have to pass through miles of forest. *Dark, shadowy forest,* Tink thought with a shiver, *where I could run into a tree snake or an owl or some other scary creature. A monster that could snap a fairy up in a single bite...*

Tink shook her head. What was

wrong with her? She had never been afraid of the forest before. Back in the days of Peter Pan, she had lived for adventures like this.

But so many things had gone wrong this time – the possums, the compass, the balloon carrier. She had made many mistakes. Maybe she had been wrong to come on this journey by herself.

Tink stood and brushed away the thought. "I just need something to eat," she told herself. "After a snack, I'll feel fit as a fiddlehead fern again."

Downstream, she spotted a gooseberry bush heavy with plump glossy berries. She flew over to it.

Tink was wrestling with a gooseberry, trying to tug it from its stem, when she suddenly had the feeling she was being watched.

She dropped the berry and ducked into the bush. Her encounter with the possums was fresh in her mind. She scanned the forest. Not a single leaf moved. Even the air was still. There was nothing –

No, wait! There! A pair of fox ears poked up from behind a hollow log.

Tink gasped. A fox would eat a fairy if it was hungry enough. Her muscles tensed. She prepared to dart away.

The ears lifted. But they weren't attached to a fox. Beneath them was the face of a boy.

"Slightly!" Tink cried.

Slightly held his finger to his lips. But it was too late. There was a flash of green as something swooped down from above.

And before them stood Peter Pan.

8

Tink grinned. Even though they'd had their ups and downs, she was always glad to see Peter. She came out from the bush and flew to meet him.

"Tink!" Peter exclaimed. "You're just in time." It had been weeks since they'd last seen each other, but Peter acted as if Tink had been away for minutes. "I was about to find Slightly," he told her.

"Were not!" came the voice from behind the log. "At least, not until Tink gave me away." Slightly poked his head up to scowl at Tink.

Peter reached over and tapped Slightly on the head. "And now you're it."

At the word "it," there was a rustle in the bushes. Cubby, Nibs, and the

Twins came out from their hiding places.

Tink looked over the boys in their ragged animal-fur suits. Someone was missing.

"Where's Tootles?" she asked Peter.

Peter shrugged. "Sometimes he falls asleep." He jumped onto a tree branch and leaned out past the leaves. "Tootles! Tootles, come out!" he called.

There was no reply.

"Tootles! Tootles!" the Lost Boys called. But still they heard nothing.

Suddenly, one of the Twins cried out. "Peter, look! Tootles's footprints go to here. Then they disappear!"

Peter leaped down to study the tracks. He whistled low. "Disappeared right into thin air. There's only one thing that could have happened."

The boys stared at him, wide-eyed.

"Tootles has been *kidnapped!*" Peter declared.

Tink gasped. She was not overly fond of Tootles. He had always tried to catch her and stuff her into his pockets. But – kidnapped!

Peter turned to the Lost Boys. "Men, we must rescue Tootles. But it may be dangerous." His eyes twinkled. This was just the sort of adventure he adored. "Only the bravest among you may go with me," he told the boys.

The Lost Boys all wanted to be the bravest. They scrambled to line up behind him.

Tink hesitated. Peter looked back at her. "Aren't you coming, Tink?"

He smiled his reckless smile. It

suddenly seemed as if no time had passed since her days with Peter Pan. Swept up in the excitement, Tink forgot all about her search for the pixie dust.

"Of course I'm coming!" she cried.

"Then let's go!" said Peter.

They set off marching through the forest. Tink flew in front. They hadn't gone far, though, when she cried out. Peter stopped short. The boys behind him bumped into each other.

Tink flew down and landed next to a paw print in the mud.

"Tracks! Good job, Tink," Peter said. He knelt beside her to look at the track. "It belongs to a tiger. A big one, from the look of it!"

They found another paw print not far off. Tink, Peter, and the boys followed the tracks. They circled right back to the place where Tootles's tracks ended.

"Oh, no." Suddenly, Tink figured out what had happened. She looked at Peter, her eyes wide.

Peter shook his head sadly. "Poor Tootles has been eaten by a tiger."

The Twins' mouths fell open at the same time. Cubby turned as pale as a fish's belly. All the boys stared at Peter.

"Bow your heads, fellas," Peter instructed. "Poor old Tootles."

With loud sniffles the Lost Boys lowered their heads. Tink landed on Peter's shoulder and solemnly dimmed her glow.

Peter began a little speech. "We'll never forget Tootles. He was a deadeye with a slingshot."

"Aye," said Cubby, "except when he missed."

Peter went on. "Our friend Tootles was a – "

Rrrrow! Suddenly, they heard a loud growl above them.

"The tiger!" Cubby shrieked. He tried to run, but he tripped over the Twins. All three landed in a heap.

Tink flew up into the tree branches. She began to laugh. "That's no tiger," she said. "It's Tootles!"

The growl came again. Now everyone could tell it wasn't a tiger's roar. It was only Tootles's hungry stomach.

"What are you doing?" Peter asked him.

Tootles looked down from the rope that held him. "Hiding," he replied. "I think I found the best hiding spot."

A few days before, Peter and the Lost Boys had rigged the trap, hoping to catch a tiger. Tootles had stumbled into it by mistake when he was looking for a hiding place.

The boys weren't fooled. "Ha-ha!" Slightly laughed. "Tootles got caught in a tiger trap! Tootles got caught in a tiger trap!"

The other boys took up the cry. "Tootles got caught in a tiger trap!"

Peter flew up to the tree branch. He drew his knife to cut down the rope. As he did, they heard a low, deep growl. All heads swiveled to look at Tootles.

"Wasn't me," Tootles said with a shrug.

"The tiger!" Peter cried, just as a huge beast sprang from the bushes.

Up in the air, Tootles, Peter, and Tink were safe. But the tiger was headed straight for the other Lost Boys.

Without thinking, Tink snatched her sack of fairy dust and turned it upside down over them. "Fly!" she yelled.

They didn't waste a second. The Lost Boys leaped into the air. They just missed being caught in the tiger's claws.

The boys perched in the branches of the surrounding trees. On the ground, the tiger prowled from trunk to trunk. It twitched its tail and watched them with yellow eyes. But they were out of its reach.

"Can't catch us!" Peter cried at the tiger.

"Nyah, nyah! Can't catch us, tiger!" the other boys echoed. They snatched small fruits from the branches around them and threw them at the big cat.

Annoyed, the tiger finally slunk away. When they were sure it was gone, Peter cut Tootles down.

Slightly puffed up his chest. "We sure showed that tiger!" he declared.

"Nah! If it wasn't for Tink, you'd have been his dinner," Peter told him.

The boys knew it was true. They all turned to look at Tink. "Hooray for Tinker Bell!" they cheered. Tink's glow turned pink as she blushed.

"She should get an award for bravery," Peter said. He fished around in his pocket. At last he came up with a golden bead the size of a small pea. He threaded a piece of grass through it and hung it around Tink's neck.

"We present this medal to Tinker

Bell," he announced, "the best and bravest fairy in Never Land."

Tink's heart swelled. Why had she ever doubted herself? She was the best and bravest fairy. And she could still prove it!

"Peter, I have to fly to the Northern Shore," she said. "Can you tell me how far it is?"

"Maybe a half day's flight," Peter replied. "Aw, Tink, don't you want to stick around and play?"

Tink smiled and checked the bag of fairy dust. There was still a little left in the bottom. Enough to take her the rest of the way.

"I'll see you again soon," she told Peter. She waved to the Lost Boys. Then, clutching her medal to her chest, she set out once again for the Northern Shore.

9

By sunset, Tink was weary from flying. But her spirits were high. The wind had grown chilly, and she smelled salt in the air. She felt sure she was close to the Northern Shore.

The sky faded from purple to black. The wind blew harder and grew colder still. It numbed her ears and her hands. Tink thought longingly of the sweater she'd lost in the balloon carrier.

A fat, round moon rose. Back in Pixie Hollow, the Fairy Dance would be starting. Tink imagined her friends gathering in the fairy circle, wearing their finest clothes. She could almost hear the music and the laughter. For a moment, she wished she were there.

But she couldn't give up now.

She went over a crest. Ahead, the ground dropped away into ocean. Waves pounded the rocks on the shore.

The Northern Shore! Tink marveled. *I made it! I made it!*

There could be no doubt about it this time. A glowing silver cloud hovered in the air, just above the water. *It's the cloud of pixie dust*, Tink thought. *Just like in Tor's story.*

Tink beat the air with her wings. Within moments, she was skimming the water. The sound of the surf roared in her ears. Spray from the crashing waves soaked her from head to toe.

But where was the pixie dust?

She hovered, looking this way and that. But the air was misty and damp.

She couldn't see far. Her wings began to grow heavy with the salt spray.

Looking down, she saw the water churning against the rocks below. A cold jolt of fear shot through her. If she fell, she would be swallowed by the waves.

Quickly, Tink darted back to shore. She found a dry nook high on the side of a rock. From her spot, she once again looked for the pixie dust. There it was!

Just then, a cloud passed across the moon. Before Tink's eyes, the pixie dust changed. It no longer seemed to glow. And it wasn't really silver; it was...

"It's nothing but mist!" Tink's voice trembled. What she had taken for a cloud of pixie dust was only spray from the surf, shining in the moonlight.

That couldn't be right. Surely she

was in the wrong spot. There had to be another cloud – the real cloud of pixie dust. There had to!

Tink scoured the coastline with her eyes. But there wasn't a cloud to be seen.

"I came all this way for nothing," she said. "I… I failed."

Her legs wobbled. She had to clutch the side of the rock to keep from falling. She had never failed before. Not like this.

Finally, she recovered enough to stand. She ripped the medal Peter had given her from her neck and eyed it scornfully.

"Best," she sneered. "I'm not the best at anything."

She didn't even have the energy to throw it. Tink opened her hand and let it fall. The bead bounced once off the side of the rock and sank into the ocean.

Tink flew slowly back through the forest toward Pixie Hollow. When she became too tired to go on, she found a large flower and curled up in its petals for a few minutes of rest. But she never slept. Thoughts swirled through her mind like leaves caught in a whirlpool.

After all her effort, she had nothing to give Terence. "He will never want to be my friend now," Tink murmured.

She knew she should fly quickly. She was running low on fairy dust. If it ran out, she might never make it back home. But Tink was in no hurry. What did she have to look forward to?

As Tink pondered this, she heard a crashing sound not far away. It was followed by a thud.

Someone groaned, "Oh, no."

Tink darted around a fig tree and through a tangle of vines. She spotted a big hole in the ground. She crept to the edge and peeped in.

There was Tootles staring back at her.

"Tink!" he cried happily.

"What are you doing down there?" asked Tink.

"Oh." Tootles blushed. "I fell into another trap. We dug this one last week. Peter said we'd catch a bear. Only, it looks like we caught me instead."

"Foolish boy," said Tink.

Tootles nodded. He was used to being called foolish, among other things.

"Can you give me some fairy dust to fly out?" he asked.

Tink rolled her eyes. She was really too busy to be looking after this silly boy. *Then again*, she thought with a sigh, *I can't just leave him to the wild animals.*

Tink had only the fairy dust left on her wings. There wasn't enough to help Tootles fly out of the hole. Looking around, she spotted a long, thick vine hanging from a nearby tree. Flapping her wings with all her might, she tugged the end of the vine to the hole. She threw it over the edge.

Tootles grabbed it, and he pulled himself out. He sat on the edge of the hole, huffing and puffing. "Promise not to tell Peter?" he asked when he'd caught his breath.

Tink had no intention of making such a promise. If Peter had been there, she would have told him at once. As it was, she said nothing.

Tootles took her silence as a yes. "Tinker Bell, you should have an award for bravery," he said. He was trying his best to sound like Peter.

He reached into his pockets. But all he found were a few pebbles. Nothing that could be used as a medal.

Tootles scratched his head. His fingers found a sparrow's feather he'd stuck in his cap. As a rule, Peter did not allow the Lost Boys to wear feathers in their caps, since he wore one himself. But this feather was so tiny and insignificant, it had escaped Peter's notice.

Solemnly, Tootles held out the feather to Tink.

Tink took it. She turned it over in her hands. "It's nothing but a sparrow's feather."

Tootles shrugged. "It's the best thing I've got," he said. "I hope you'll take good care of it." With a wave, he ran off to find the other boys.

Tink stood for a moment, looking at the feather. Then she leaped up and began to fly toward home. She knew what she had to do.

10

T<small>INK GOT BACK</small> to Pixie Hollow just before dinnertime. As she neared the Home Tree kitchen, she smelled chestnuts roasting. Her mouth watered. For two days, she'd had nothing to eat but berries.

But Tink flew on. There was something she had to do first.

When she reached her workshop, Tink stopped short in surprise. Terence, Silvermist, Iridessa, Rosetta, and Fawn were standing outside her door.

Tink hovered uncertainly. She had known she would have to face everyone eventually. But she hadn't expected to do it so soon. What are they doing here? she wondered.

They were waiting for her, of course. Terence had been the first to notice she was missing. When she hadn't shown up for the Fairy Dance, he'd gone to Tink's friends. But none of them had seen her. After searching all over Pixie Hollow, they had settled down by her workshop to wait. And to worry.

If Tink was startled to see them, they were even more surprised by the sight of her. They had never seen Tink in such a state! Her dress was torn. Her arms were scratched. Wisps of hair straggled from her ponytail.

The four fairies rushed over.

"Tink, where have you been?" cried Silvermist.

"We've been so worried!" Rosetta added.

"What happened to you?" asked Fawn.

Normally, Tink didn't like to be fussed over. But she was relieved to get such a warm reception. She let them hug her and brush the twigs from her hair.

As Tink's friends surrounded her, Terence hung back. He wasn't sure she would be glad to see him.

"Tink, what you need is a hot bath," said Silvermist. "I'll bring you some warm water."

"You need food," said Iridessa. "How does sunflower soup sound?"

"You'll feel much better in a new dress," said Rosetta. "And I have the perfect thing! I'll be back before you can say 'gorgeous.'"

"You need a nap!" said Fawn. "You

can borrow my fluffy feather pillow."

The four fairies flew off. Terence started to follow them.

"Terence, wait," Tink said.

She couldn't give him dust from the Pixie Dust Tree. But she could give him something. And now Tink understood that the gift wasn't important. What mattered was how it was given.

She went to the shelf in her workshop and took down the silver bowl. She placed it in Terence's hands.

"It's a perfect repair," he said. "You can't even tell it was bent. You're the best pots-and-pans fairy around, Tink." He started to hand it back.

But Tink shook her head. "It's for you."

"Why?" Terence asked, startled.

"For being my friend," said Tink.

"Friend? But… I've been trying not to be your friend. You told me to leave you alone."

Now Tink laughed. Terence thought about how he loved her laugh. It sounded like little silver bells ringing.

"I didn't mean for *good!*" she exclaimed. "I was upset. But I'm not anymore. I've been all over Never Land looking for the perfect present for you." She pointed to the bowl. "It was my first fix ever. I hope you'll take good care of it."

Finally, Terence understood. The bowl might have looked like just a silver bowl, but coming from Tink, it was much more than that. It was an apology.

He smiled. "I know just the place for it."

Then, to Tink's surprise, he flew over and placed it back on her shelf. He didn't need the bowl. Tink's friendship was all he'd ever wanted.

"I think it will be safe here," he told Tink. "And I can come by to visit it. Now, you look like you need something to eat. Shall we go to dinner?"

Tink laughed. She was messy and covered in dust, but it didn't matter. She took Terence's hand. And together the two friends flew out into the evening.